MY FIRST BOOK ABOUT OKLAHOMA

by Carole Marsh

This activity book has material which correlates with Oklahoma's Priority Academic Student Skills. At every opportunity, we have tried to relate information to the History and Social Science, English, Science, Math, Civics, Economics, and Computer Technology PASS directives. For additional information, go to our websites: www.oklahomaexperience.com or www.gallopade.com.

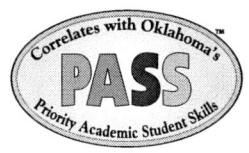  

Permission is hereby granted to the individual purchaser or classroom teacher to reproduce materials in this book for non-commercial individual or classroom use only. Reproduction of these materials for an entire school or school system is strictly prohibited.

Gallopade is proud to be a member of these educational organizations and associations:

The Oklahoma Experience Series

The Oklahoma Experience! Paperback Book

My First Pocket Guide to Oklahoma!

The Big Oklahoma Reproducible Activity Book

The Oklahoma Coloring Book!

My First Book About Oklahoma!

Oklahoma "Jography!": A Fun Run Through Our State

Oklahoma Jeopardy: Answers and Questions About Our State

The Oklahoma Experience! Sticker Pack

The Oklahoma Experience! Poster/Map

Discover Oklahoma CD-ROM

Oklahoma "GEO" Bingo Game

Oklahoma "HISTO" Bingo Game

A Word... From the Author

Do you know when I think children should start learning about their very own state? When they're born! After all, even when you're a little baby, this is your state too! This is where you were born. Even if you move away, this will always be your "home state." And if you were not born here, but moved here—this is still your state as long as you live here.

We know people love their country. Most people are very patriotic. We fly the U.S. flag. We go to Fourth of July parades. But most people also love their state. Our state is like a mini-country to us. We care about its places and people and history and flowers and birds.

As a child, we learn about our little corner of the world. Our room. Our home. Our yard. Our street. Our neighborhood. Our town. Even our county.

But very soon, we realize that we are part of a group of neighbor towns that make up our great state! Our newspaper carries stories about our state. The TV news is about happenings in our state. Our state's sports teams are our favorites. We are proud of our state's main tourist attractions.

From a very young age, we are aware that we are a part of our state. This is where our parents pay taxes and vote and where we go to school. BUT, we usually do not get to study about our state until we are in school for a few years!

So, this book is an introduction to our great state. It's just for you right now. Why wait to learn about your very own state? It's an exciting place and reading about it now will give you a head start for that time when you "officially" study our state history! Enjoy,

Carole Marsh

Oklahoma
Let's Make Words!

Make as many words as you can from the letters in the words:

OKLAHOMA, THE SOONER STATE

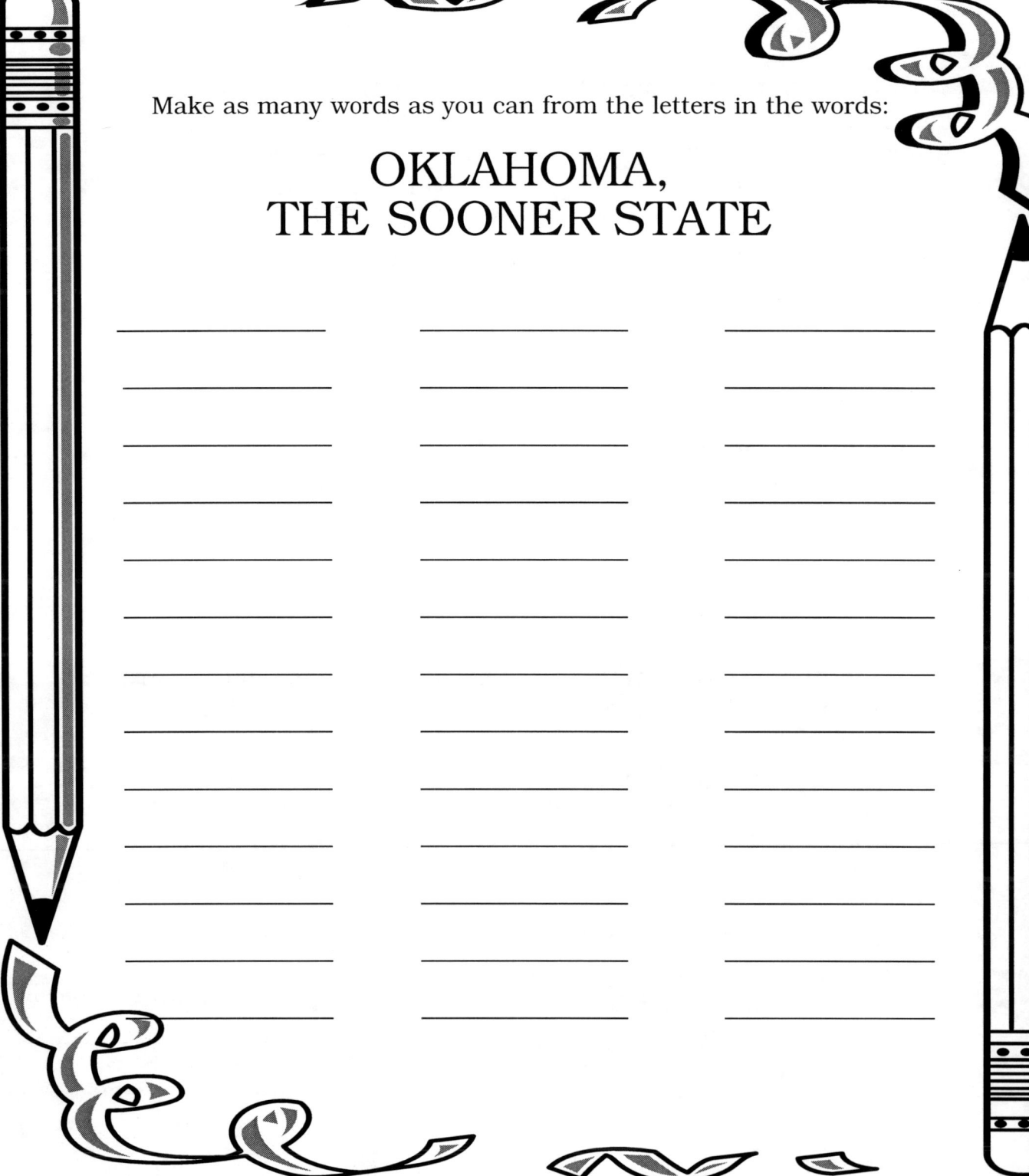

Oklahoma
The 46th State

Do you know when Oklahoma became a state? Oklahoma became the 46th state on November 16, 1907.

Color Oklahoma red. Color the Atlantic and the Pacific Ocean blue. Color the rest of the U.S. states shown here green.

©2001 Carole Marsh/Gallopade International/800-536-2GET/www.oklahomaexperience.com/Page 5

Oklahoma State Flag

The state flag of Oklahoma was adopted in 1925. It shows a buckskin shield of an Osage warrior centered on a blue background. An olive branch and a peace pipe cross the shield. On the shield are small crosses that represent stars or Oklahoma's quest for excellency. Across the bottom of the shield is the word "Oklahoma" which was added in 1941.

Color the Oklahoma flag below.

I pledge allegiance...

Oklahoma State Bird

Most states have a state bird. It should remind us that we need to "fly high" to achieve our goals. The Oklahoma state bird is the Scissor-tailed Flycatcher. Its black and white tail resembles a pair of scissors. It is gray with light orange coloring beneath its wings.

Circle your state bird, then color all the birds.

MOCKINGBIRD

SCISSOR-TAILED FLYCATCHER

CARDINAL

EAGLE

ROBIN

QUAIL

The early bird gets the worm! Yikes!

Oklahoma
State Seal and Motto

The Oklahoma state seal shows a five-pointed star surrounded by a group of golden stars. Also, on the seal is Oklahoma's state motto, *Labor omnia vincit*, which is Latin for "Labor conquers all things."

In 25 words or less, explain what this motto means:

_____

_____

_____

_____

Color the state seal.

...with liberty and justice for all!

Oklahoma State Flower

The Oklahoma state flower emblem is Mistletoe. Mistletoe has dark green leaves and bears white berries that can be seen in the fall and winter in the southern part of the state. Adopted as the state flower emblem in 1893, Mistletoe is especially popular during the winter holidays when it's traditional to be kissed underneath its hanging boughs.

Color the picture of our state flower.

Oklahoma State Tree

Our state tree reminds us that our roots should run deep if we want to grow straight and tall! Oklahoma's state tree is the Redbud. Its dark pink blossoms bloom throughout early spring. It is commonly found in Oklahoma's valleys and gorges.

Finish drawing the redbud tree, then color it.

WOW!

Oklahoma State Zoo

The Oklahoma City Zoological Park is the oldest zoo in the Southwest. Located on 110 acres (44 hectares), this fun-filled zoo is one of the best in the nation and has over 2,800 of the world's most exotic animals. Let's GO!

Match the name of the zoo animal with its picture.

Zebra

Giraffe

Monkey

Bear

Tiger

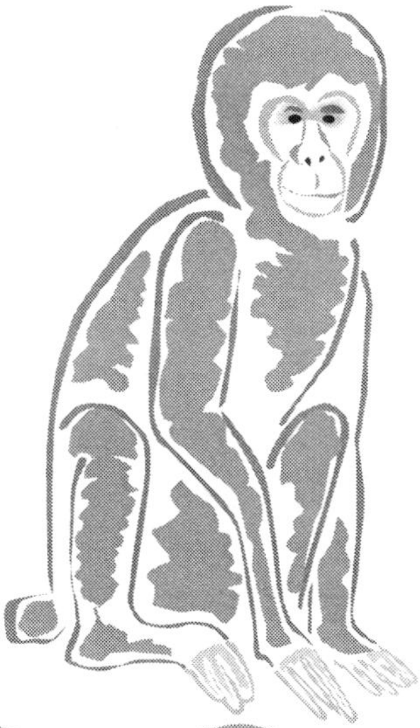

Oklahoma
State Explorers

Spanish conquistadors were the first Europeans to visit Oklahoma. In 1541, Francisco Vásquez de Coronado traveled across western Oklahoma in search of the Seven Cities of Cíbola, Cale, and Quivira. Hoping to find wealthy kingdoms, Coronado was disappointed when he found Quivira in what is now Kansas. In 1601, Juan de Oñate led Spanish settlers from their settlements on the Río Grande north to the Arkansas River and south into the Wichita Mountains.

Color the things an explorer might have used.

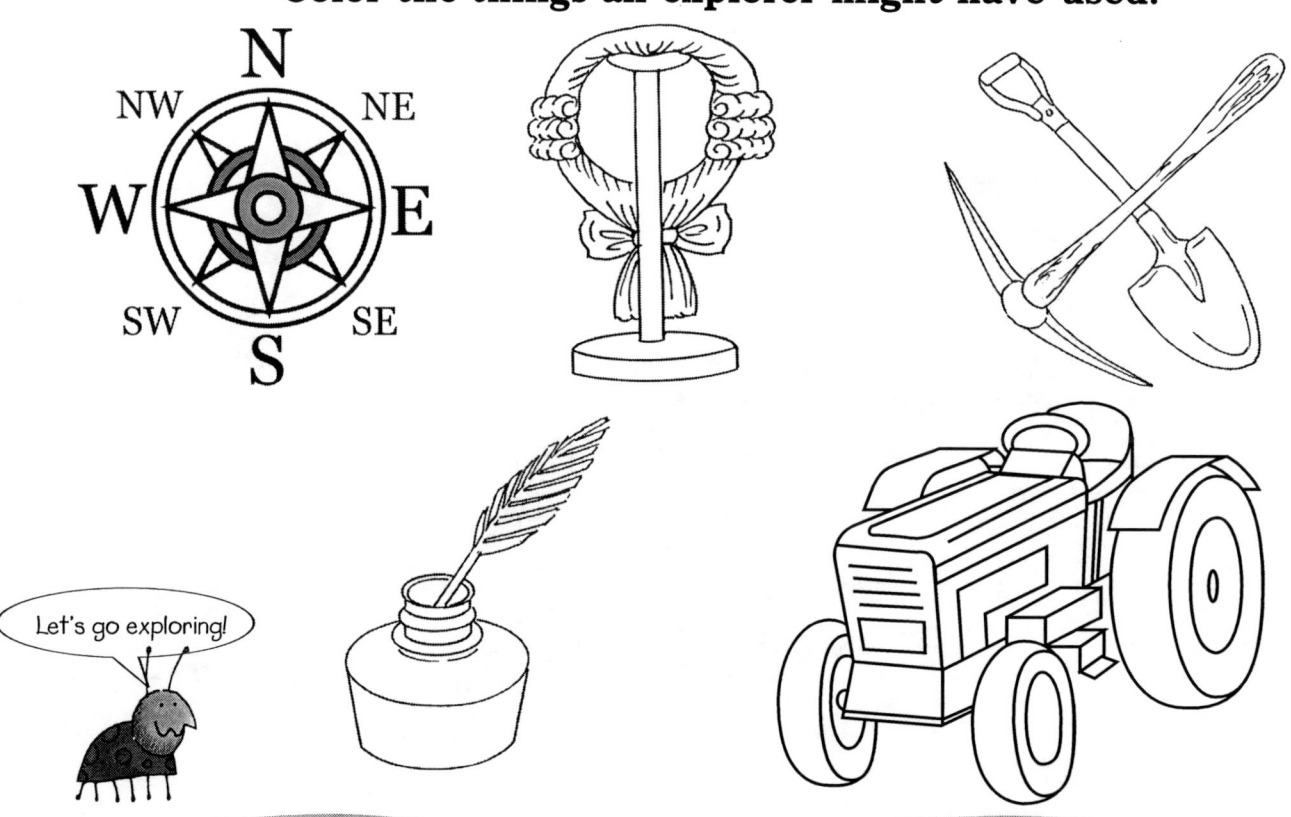

Oklahoma State Reptile

The Oklahoma state reptile is the Mountain Boomer Lizard. These lizards are members of the iguana family and are also known as Ring-necked Lizards. Their body is a shade of turquoise, and their head and neck are bright yellow with two black markings around their collar. These colorful creatures are known to run on their hind legs.

Put an X by each critter that is <u>not</u> a Mountain Boomer Lizard and then color them all!

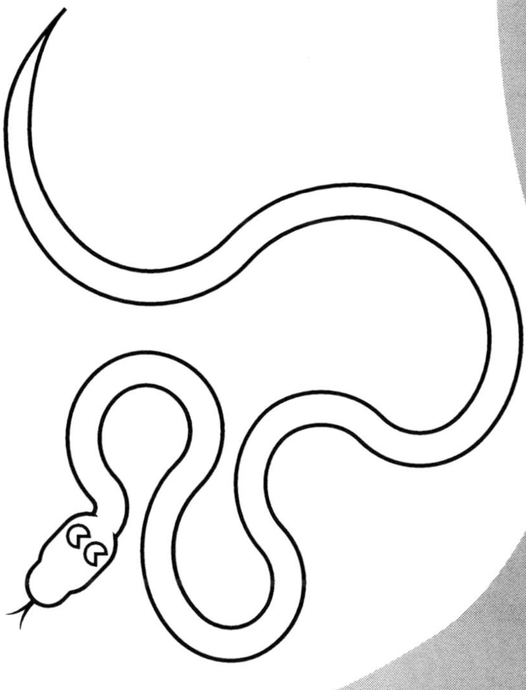

Oklahoma
One Day I Can Vote!

When you are 18 and register according to state laws, you can vote! So please do! Your vote counts!

Your friend is running for a class office.

She gets 41 votes!

Here is her opponent!

He gets 16 votes!

ANSWER THE FOLLOWING QUESTIONS:

1. Who won? ❏ friend   ❏ opponent

2. How many votes were cast altogether?

3. How many votes did the winner win by?

©2001 Carole Marsh/Gallopade International/800-536-2GET/www.oklahomaexperience.com/Page 14

Oklahoma State Capital

In 1910, the state *capital* of Oklahoma was changed from Guthrie to Oklahoma City. Until the new *capitol* building was completed in 1917, the state was governed from the Lee-Huckins Hotel. *Did you notice the different spelling?*

Add your hometown to the map. Now add other towns you have visited to the map.

(CHECK & SEE IF YOU SPELLED THEM CORRECTLY!)

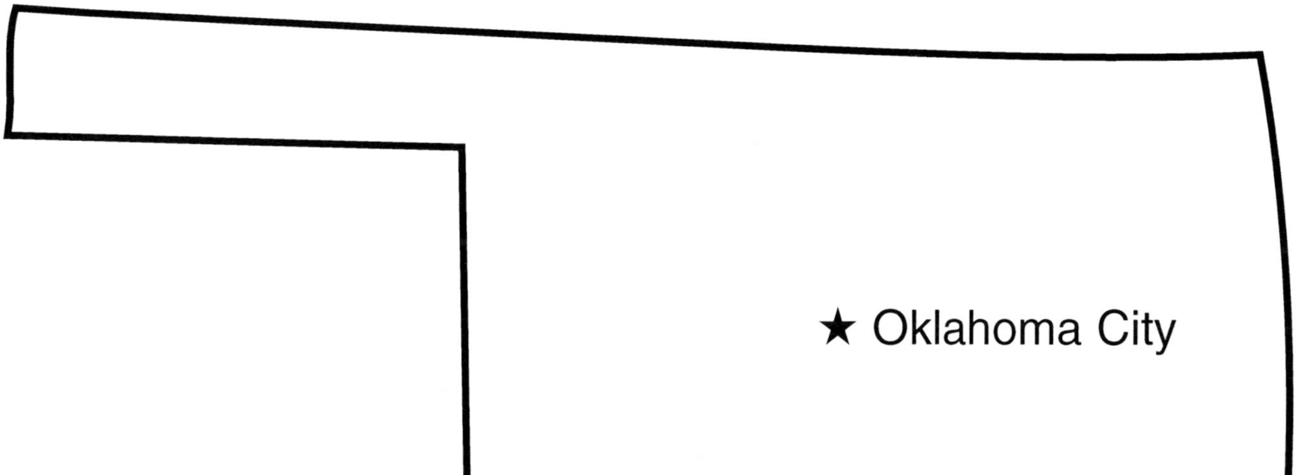

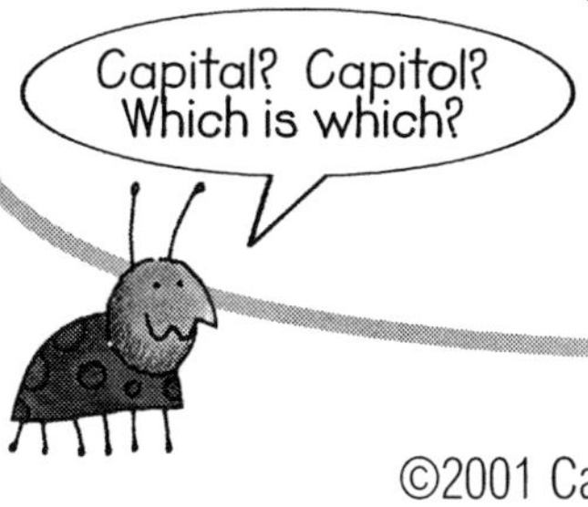

★ Oklahoma City

Capital? Capitol? Which is which?

One word: Dictionary

Oklahoma Governor

The governor of Oklahoma is the state's leader.
Do some research to complete the biography of the governor.

Governor's name:
_____

Paste a picture of the governor in the box.

The governor was born in this state:
_____

The governor has been in office since:
_____

Names of the governor's family members:
_____
_____
_____

Interesting facts about the governor:
_____
_____
_____
_____
_____

Oklahoma Crops

Some families in Oklahoma make their living from the land. Some of our state's crops or agricultural products are:

WORD BANK

nursery products   wheat   watermelons
strawberries   cotton   cattle

UNSCRAMBLE THESE IMPORTANT STATE CROPS

ectlat _____   atweh _____

brsertswaire _____   ttnooc _____

lwmtraeenos _____   yenrusr dpourstc _____ _____

Oklahoma State Holidays

These are just some of the holidays that Oklahoma celebrates.

Number these holidays in order from the beginning of the year.

Columbus Day 2nd Monday in October	Thanksgiving 4th Thursday in November	Presidents' Day 3rd Monday in February
Independence Day July 4	Labor Day first Monday in September	New Year's Day January 1
Memorial Day last Monday in May	Veterans Day November 11	Christmas December 25

Oklahoma Nickname

Oklahoma has a very special nickname. It is called the Sooner State. It is called that because of the would-be landowners who snuck into the Oklahoma territory "sooner" than everyone else to claim potential tracts of land. Federal troops marched the over-eager "sooners" back to the border.

What other nicknames would suit our state and why?

_____
_____
_____
_____

What nicknames would suit your town or your school?

_____
_____
_____
_____
_____

Oklahoma
How BIG is Our State?

Our state is the 20th largest state in the United States. It has an area of 69,903 square miles (181,048 square kilometers).

Can you answer the following questions?

1. How many states are there in the United States?
   _____

2. This many states are smaller than our state:
   _____

3. This many states are larger than our state:
   _____

4. One mile = 5,280 ____ ____ ____ ____

   HINT:

5. Draw a picture of a "square" mile.

ANSWERS: 1-50; 2-30; 3-19; 4-feet; 5- ☐

Oklahoma People

A state is not just towns and mountains and rivers. A state is its people! Some really important people in a state are not always famous. You may know them—they may be your mom, your dad, or your teacher. The average, everyday person is the one who makes the state a good state. How? By working hard, by paying taxes, by voting, and by helping Oklahoma children grow up to be good state citizens!

Match each Oklahoma person with their accomplishment.

1. Ralph Waldo Ellison
2. Geronimo
3. Mickey Mantle
4. Zebulon Pike
5. Will Rogers
6. Sequoyah
7. Alice Mary Robertson
8. Maria Tallchief

A. famous entertainer and humorist
B. played baseball for the New York Yankees
C. fierce Apache warrior imprisoned at Fort Still
D. American classical ballerina
E. Cherokee leader who created an alphabet
F. distinguished African-American author
G. female member of the U.S. House of Representatives
H. explorer who traveled across Oklahoma

ANSWERS: 1-F; 2-C; 3-B; 4-H; 5-A; 6-E; 7-G; 8-D

Oklahoma Gazetteer

A gazetteer is a list of places.

Use the word bank to complete the names of some of these famous places in our state:

1. _ _ _ _ _ _ Mountain

2. Winding _ _ _ _ _ Mountain National Recreation Area

3. National _ _ _ _ _ _ Hall of Fame and Western Heritage Center

4. Tom _ _ _ Museum

5. The _ _ _ _ _ _ Gardens

6. The _ _ _ _ Homestead

7. The Oklahoma Air _ _ _ _ _ Museum

8. The _ _ _ _ _ _ _ _ City Memorial

9. Wolf's _ _ _ _ _ _

10. The Mansion of Mattie _ _ _ _

WORD BANK
Stair   Harn
Beal   Mix
Quartz   Oklahoma
Cowboy   Space
Heaven   Myriad

ANSWERS: 1-Quartz; 2-Stair; 3-Cowboy; 4-Mix; 5-Myriad; 6-Harn; 7-Space; 8-Oklahoma; 9-Heaven; 10-Beal

Oklahoma Neighbors

No person or state lives alone. You have neighbors where you live. Sometimes they may be right next door. Other times, they may be way down the road. But you live in the same neighborhood and are interested in what goes on there.

You have neighbors at school. The children who sit in front, beside, or behind you are your neighbors. You may share books. You might borrow a pencil. They might ask you to move so they can see the board better.

We have a lot in common with our state neighbors. Some of our land is alike. We share some history. We care about our part of the country. We share borders. Some of our people go there; some of their people come here. Most of the time we get along with our state neighbors. Even when we argue or disagree, it is a good idea for both of us to work it out. After all, states are not like people—they can't move away!

Use the color key to color Oklahoma and its neighbors.

Color Key:

Oklahoma-blue
Kansas-green
Arkansas-red
Texas-orange
Colorado-yellow
New Mexico-purple
Missouri-brown

Oklahoma Highs and Lows

The highest point in Oklahoma is Black Mesa. Black Mesa reaches 4,973 feet (1,516 meters) into the sky!

Draw a family climbing Black Mesa.

The lowest point in Oklahoma is Little River in McCurtain County. Little River is 287 feet (87 meters) above sea level.

Draw a boating scene on the Little River.

Oklahoma
Old Man River

Oklahoma has many great rivers. Rivers give us water for our crops. Rivers are also water "highways." On these water highways travel crops, manufactured goods, people, and many other things—including children in tire tubes!

Here are some of Oklahoma's most important rivers:

Arkansas	**Illinois**
Red	**Poteau**
Cimarron	**North Fork**
Canadian	**Washita**
Grand	**Kiamichi**

Draw a kid "tubing" down the Oklahoma River!

Oklahoma Weather ... Or Not!

What kind of climate does our state have?

- Most of Oklahoma has very hot, long summers.
- Most of Oklahoma has moderate, short winters.
- January temperatures for Oklahoma usually average around -27°F (-32°C).
- May through September temperatures for Oklahoma usually average around lower 100s°F (upper 30s°C).

What is the weather outside now? Draw a picture.

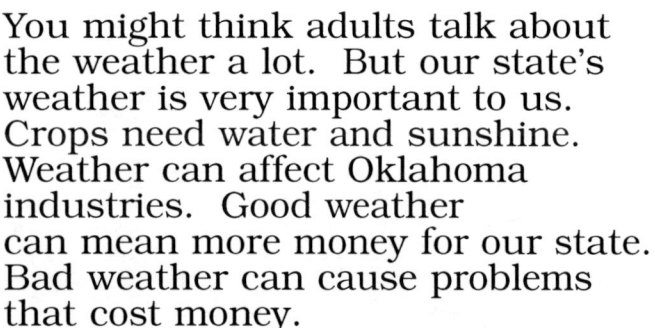

You might think adults talk about the weather a lot. But our state's weather is very important to us. Crops need water and sunshine. Weather can affect Oklahoma industries. Good weather can mean more money for our state. Bad weather can cause problems that cost money.

ACTIVITY: Do you watch the nightly news at your house? If you do, you might see the weather report. Tonight, turn on the weather report. The reporter often talks about our state's regions, cities, towns, and our neighboring states. Watching the weather report is a great way to learn about our state. It also helps you to know what to wear to school tomorrow!

Oklahoma Indian Tribes

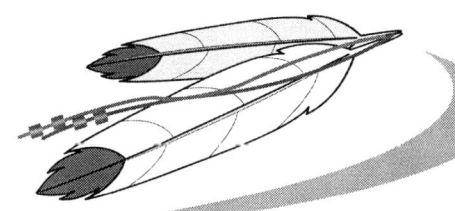

The American Indians were first on our land, long before it was a state. Oklahoma's main Indian tribes include:

Historic Tribes
Wichita
Caddo
Quapaw
Kiowa Apache

Five Civilized Tribes
Choctaw
Chickasaw
Creek
Seminole
Cherokee

Help Maize find her way through the maize (corn) field maze to her teepee!

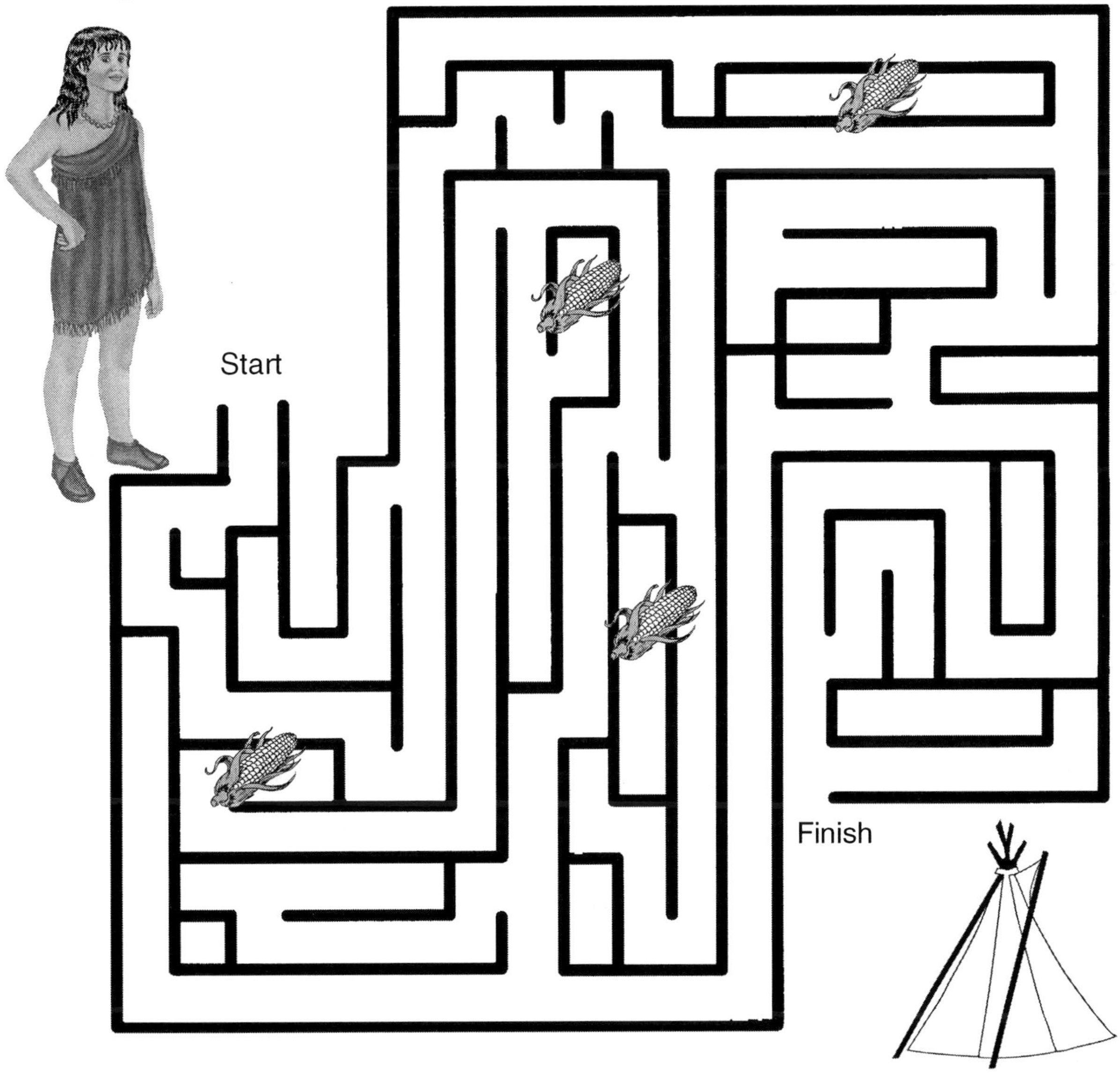

Start

Finish

©2001 Carole Marsh/Gallopade International/800-536-2GET/www.oklahomaexperience.com/Page 27

Oklahoma Website Page

Here is a website you can go to and learn more about Oklahoma:
www.state.ok.us

Design your own state website page on the computer screen below.

Oklahoma
State Animal

Oklahoma's state animal is the American Buffalo, sometimes called Bison. These large animals once roamed freely across the southern plains. Buffalos have dark brown, shaggy coats and large heads. They stand almost 6 feet (1.8 meters) tall and can weigh close to 2,000 pounds (907 kilograms).

Color the American Buffalo below.

Oklahoma State Fish

Oklahoma's state fish is the White or Sand Bass. It is a dark blue-green fish with silvery sides. It has a white belly and black stripes along the length of its body. It lives in the large lakes and rivers of Oklahoma and is an excellent game fish.

Draw six fish in the water below. Color each one a different color.

Oklahoma Spelling Bee!

What's All The Buzz About?

Here are some words related to Oklahoma.

See if you can find them in the Word Search below.

WORD LIST

| STATE | RIVER | PEOPLE | TREE | BIRD |
| FLAG | VOTE | FLOWER | SONG | INSECT |

```
A X N Y H N V S D G T R E P
V O T E M A C S E A B A Y E
S N B R X B R K S X B D S O
Y B P Q L S O N G R I J H P
R I V E R P P L R T Y U E L
Q R E R R Y Z E E R T O N E
R D P P A E A O N E C K A R
S X O C E A W C T C E S N I
P O B U Y U Y O E O L L D O
Q U F L A G R K L L X Z O P
Z X R D G H R E U F L L A L
M R D W Q N M N S T A T E Z
```

Oklahoma Trivia

I ♥ Oklahoma!

In the winter, more than two million migratory ducks, geese, and other waterfowl make Sequoyah National Wildlife Refuge near Vian their home.

A Rattlesnake Derby is held each April in Mangum.

The 12 earthen mounds in LeFlore County have often been called the "King Tut of the West."

Comanche was the name of Will Rogers' favorite quarterhorse.

Woodward Elks Rodeo is known as "the toughest rodeo in Oklahoma."

The first Red Cross canteen was established in El Reno. It provided meals, cigarettes, writing paper, and hospitality to World War I soldiers.

Oklahoma's first post office was established in 1824 at the Miller Courthouse.

William Wrigley manufactured his first package of chewing gum in Guthrie.

The Choctaw Indian word *Oklahoma* means "red people."

Now, add a fact you know about Oklahoma here:
_____
_____
_____